This is definitely a work of fiction
and dedicated to my wife, Fatima, who made
me write it.

PROLOGUE

It is 2010, just over a year since Great Britain became an Islamic emirates, ushering in a controversial chapter in the country's long history as a global power. How this inconceivable event happened remains a matter of debate, but, according to historians favourable of the emirates, it all unravelled before the British forces returned home from a tour of duty in Iraq.

In 2008, a year before Britain pulled its armed forces out of Iraq, an Iraq-based battalion captured Sheikh Ahmed Hussayn, the spiritual leader of an Iraqi insurgency group, following fierce fighting in a town south of Iraq. He was held at an Iraqi police station, a makeshift interrogation centre where commanding officer Lieutenant Colonel Richard Bailey realised that this was no ordinary cleric but someone of a high rank. Sheikh Ahmed's quiet confidence and absolute resolution to give nothing away created much intrigue amongst his captors.

Three days after the capture, the Colonel was astonished to hear that the sheikh had decided to cooperate and requested that he speak with him. The sheikh told him that *he* was, in fact, the leader of the insurgency group, the head of 25,000 armed fighters. To prove it he would share with him details of secrets only his most trusted captains would know; the secrets included bunkers which housed Saddam's fortunes and weapons stock pile. This checked out to be true so the sheikh made a second request: that he meet the UK's commander for the south and in return, he would reveal to him plans for all operations there and abroad. Seeing that this was a golden opportunity, and knowing he had nothing to lose, the Colonel arranged the meeting.

The sheikh was transported from the police station in a heavily armed convoy and taken to an army base several hundred miles away. There, the UK commanding officer Major General George Fraser eagerly awaited his arrival. The meeting took place between the Major General and the sheikh in a large but poorly lit room with nothing more than a table and two chairs, while a few soldiers kept guard outside. The encounter lasted three hours, and suffice it to say the Major General was a different man when he left the room. He continued to see the sheikh intermittently for a few hours a day for the next week, and over time more and more senior personnel joined him in these meetings. This continued for many weeks until the sheikh was moved from the base and transferred to the infamous Guantanamo Bay prison camp, but he never made it there and no one knew what became of him thereafter.

The story goes that the sheikh's stoic attitude and radiant charisma helped convert the Major General to Islam in their very first meeting. The Major General then converted others in his command until a sizable number of senior personnel had accepted Islam as their religion. It is said that the conversations in the meetings were not about the war but were more reflective in nature. The meetings focussed on the subordination of the ego, as shaped by the material world, and the elevation of the self to recognise a higher purpose. The conversions spread at an unprecedented rate, forming a secret movement within the British army who called themselves the Companions.

The Companions kept their new religion hidden from their non-Muslim counterparts for fear that they may be deemed a threat to the wider army. In a final address, the sheikh stated that the conversions were an act of divine providence for the purpose of influencing change when they returned home. He argued that the Companions were in a unique position to put an end to the country's meddling and bullying of other sovereign states for the simple purpose of lining the pockets of a select few. It was time the country became concerned with the care of its own people only. The sheikh stressed that, as protectors and citizens of Great Britain, this burden fell on them and them alone.

Inspired by their new religion and armed with a strong resolve to change Great Britain for the better, the Companions spent a year planning a coup d'état, believing this was the only remedial action that would save their country. The plan included recruiting and enlisting the help of members within the domestic forces. These were specific people most trusted by the Companions who signed up to their cause. Steps were shrewdly put in place to pacify noncompliant domestic forces such as the police and opposing service personnel. A long list of strategic sites were drawn up for a nationwide take over that included Parliament, security services, Government buildings, power plants, media outlets and many more.

In June 2009, four months after they returned home from Iraq, the majority of the British soldiers took part in a surprise military operation to overthrow the British Government. Being intimate with the communication lines, security and governance structures of the country, and with near unlimited access to weapons and military equipment, the Companions were able to seize power with relative success. Stealth tactics were deployed to take three out of the four countries within Great Britain with their capitals; London, Edinburgh and Cardiff were all under the complete control of the Companions and were redefined as emirates. There were many casualties and these were mainly civilians who had no idea what was going on and were caught in the crossfire. As far as they knew, the British army was locked in battle with a foreign enemy. Where possible, the Companions warned off civilians with propaganda that there had been a terrorist attack and that they should find safety and not come out until further notice. A communication blackout prevented the public at large from knowing what was really going on, removing any chances of mass panic and armed resistance.

The prime minster, the Royal Family and other Government officials were all captured and held in custody at various secret locations across London and the wider country. Without wasting any time, and to address the growing speculation, the leader of the Companions, Major General George Fraser, delivered a live victory broadcast that featured him behind a podium outside Number 10 Downing Street in full military uniform.

'In the name of Allah, the Most Gracious, the Most Merciful. The Lord of the Worlds has inspired me, Major General Muhammad

George Fraser, to create a new British governing system, and I have delivered. I assure you that, by Allah, you have nothing to fear and your lives will change only for the better.

'It is evident that our country's priorities have been completely wrong. Much focus has been on changing governments abroad when the nation at home has been crippled by austerity measures and punitive taxation. It is in need of repair for mismanagement and moral bankruptcy. The rich have become richer and the poor have become poorer. This had to change.

'Our beautiful country will now enjoy a great future protected by Allah's guidance — the laws of *shari'ah*. It is above the corruption of laws created by the whims and desires of a few self-interested men. The job at hand is a big one; there are numerous inequalities in health, income and opportunities, as well as an unaccountable political system that needs to be overhauled.

'I have already taken steps for change by appointing a new overseeing s*hari'ah* body, the House of Companions. It is made up of men and women most knowledgeable and sincere of all my colleagues, adept in all the necessary fields to move our country forward into a period of prosperity and equity.

'The House of Companions will oversee Parliament and other assemblies who I will reinstate to govern you, the non-Muslim majority in the country, as they were elected to do so. Parliament has been acquitted of all responsibilities that have led them astray — setting taxes, managing our relations abroad and protecting our borders. Instead, this burden will lie with the House of Companions.

'A small head tax, *jizya,* will be introduced. In return, each citizen will be afforded unequivocal protection, rights and liberty. Followers of the Islamic faith will be governed by Islamic Law and will be expected to pay *zakat,* a religious tax, and demonstrate exemplary citizenship to all others in society. You can expect treatment that is no better or no worse than that of your fellow non-Muslim citizens.

'As your new leader and emir, I believe that this is a path that will lead our country to unparalleled greatness and make it a beacon of light in the darkness of global challenges we face today. Thank you very much. Peace and salutations to you all.'

No sooner had the new emir finished his speech, than a dishevelled-looking prime minister, no longer detained, stepped out of Number 10 and shook the new emir's hand with an uneasy smile, concluding the transmission.

CHAPTER I

In an ACCU ward, on the third floor of the University College Hospital tower, two anaesthetists, a consultant and a specialist registrar discussed the progress of a patient at the foot of his hospital bed. Their conversation was no more than a quiet murmur in a room full of coma patients who couldn't hear them.

'This Derek Christensen chap is making remarkable progress… His CT scans show a near complete reduction in the swelling of his brain,' said the consultant, looking intently at a clipboard in his hands.

'I've not seen this before — he is a lucky fellow. His vital signs look encouraging — blood pressure normal, heart rate and oxygen all good,' added the registrar, pointing at a monitor beside Derek's bed.

'Let's keep an eye on him, but I think we can wean him off the propofol in a day or two,' the consultant said, signing the clipboard and then gently placing it at the foot of Derek's bed.

'Sure, he'll be waking up to a different world a year after his accident!' said the registrar.

Both clinicians exited the ward, leaving it to the soft beeping of various monitoring devices.

* * *

Derek Christensen, a forty-four-year-old single man, had been a black cab driver before a car accident left him hospitalised for over a year. The head injuries he'd sustained meant that an induced coma had been necessary to keep him alive. Two days after the CT scan, Derek's fingers started to twitch. True to the consultant's words, Derek was beginning to come around — but this wasn't as straightforward as someone waking from regular sleep. Derek's awareness of self and surroundings were far from normal, but he would occasionally be able to do things like squeeze the nurse's hands when asked to do so.

When asleep, Derek weaved in and out of dreams like someone was repeatedly playing him a film reel of some of his darkest moments: at breakfast a young Derek is being humiliated by his mother over his O Level results, saying that even the local 'pakis' in his class did better; in another scene Derek is arguing with a Job Centre advisor telling him that he would rather remain unemployed than work for a foreigner; but the worst memory he endured was one where he stood alone over his wife's grave, weeping profusely. The dreams continued to haunt Derek until a few days later, when a man's voice cut through them like sunlight piercing through rainclouds. The voice at first was faint but grew bold and clear, a loud pronouncement in a foreign tongue, deep and melodious. It sounded exotic but strangely familiar, captivating like an inner wake-up call encouraging him to become conscious.

'The v-voice… heavenly…' Derek mumbled his first words in a barely audible voice, his eyes flickering open.

'It's the Muslim call to prayer,' answered a nurse as she rushed over to check vitals on his monitor. 'Welcome back, Mr Christensen, welcome back!'

* * *

Two months after waking, Derek was in the hospital gym with his physiotherapist, learning how to walk again. He was now a slim chap, well over six feet tall, and it was difficult to tell that this had once been a heavily built man. Fatima, the physiotherapist, was a small Asian lady sporting a white uniform with a navy headscarf covering her hair. Though dwarfed by Derek, she was strong and didn't struggle to keep Derek upright when he stumbled in his steps.

'Your muscles are much stronger now; you've come a long way from those parallel walking bars,' she said encouragingly.

'Out of the frying pan and into the fire!' rasped Derek, trying his best to walk without any aid.

'I don't get it,' said Fatima, stopping and looking a little puzzled. 'Are you not pleased that you're leaving the hospital soon?'

'Erm, *no*. My accident was tragic, but the bigger tragedy is waking up to this nightmare — this Emirates of Britain malarkey!' cried Derek.

'I think you should focus on your recovery and take each day at a time —' said Fatima, but Derek wasn't having any of it; the fear of leaving the hospital and the changes in society was too much for him.

'The life I knew before the accident has gone, so *how* can I be expected to return to normality when our land is under Muslim control?!'

'"Under new management", I'd say, but I am sorry you feel this way,' said Fatima, patiently resuming her support for Derek's slow steps. 'Your rehabilitation has been better than expected. You could even return to your old job before you know it.'

'Yeah, you *would* say that — you're one of them!' barked Derek.

'What's that supposed to mean??' said Fatima incredulously, stopping again.

'You heard! You must be pleased *your lot* have taken over!'

'Yes, I am Muslim but *they* are not "my lot"!' snapped Fatima, her professional manner vanishing in an instant. 'I wasn't given a choice in the matter, so please do not direct your frustration at me!'

'Ok, ok, it's not your fault, exactly, but you're ok with this. I mean, would you have chosen *them* if you had the choice?'

'Honestly? There's been no big difference to my life save for women-only carriages on the underground and less morons trying to pull my hijab off on the street! Anyway, I'm not sure why you're so hostile towards it — the staff at ACCU said you woke up to a mosque *adhan* and called it "heavenly"!'

'HOW DARE YOU USE THAT AGAINST ME!' growled Derek, shaking with anger.

Startled, a few patients and their therapists stopped in their tracks and glared at Derek warily.

'I WAS DELIRIOUS BECAUSE OF ALL THE DRUGS YOU PUMPED INTO MY BODY!'

'Sorry, I apologise — I was completely out of line,' said Fatima in a soft, unequivocal tone, knowing that she had overdone it with her last remark.

'You've been kind to me so I'll let you off the hook, but it's simple… At the end of the day, you're one of them,' said Derek tartly, nodding as if he had reached some sort of conclusion. 'Just take me back to my ward, we're done here.'

CHAPTER II

Six months later, Derek was well enough to return to work as a black cabby. One warm evening, he was cruising through London's Regent Street after dropping off a customer at Oxford Circus. Piccadilly Circus was packed with tourists buzzing around, snapping their smartphones at the illuminating signs surrounding them — particularly the colourful ones advertising designer *abayas* for Muslim women. Other tourists rested at the foot of the statue of Eros on the Shaftesbury Memorial Fountain, taking selfies.

'Bloody sheep!' muttered Derek, unable to share in their good spirits. He pulled over near Glasshouse Street to let in a woman who had stuck her arm out for a cab.

The middle-aged woman in smart attire stepped into the vehicle carrying a large leather bag over one of her shoulders. She looked somewhat familiar, and asked to be taken to Parliament Square, so Derek thought this an opportune moment to spark a conversation with someone important.

'Working late, love?'

'Unfortunately, yes. I'm off to an important briefing,' replied the woman. She flashed him a smile but didn't glance up from the papers she was shuffling on her lap.

'You look familiar but I can't seem to put me finger on it,' said Derek.

'Well, I'm the MP for Poplar and Limehouse,' said the woman, now putting her papers away.

'Yes, of course. I'm from the Isle of Dogs myself. Sorry, I didn't catch your name…'

'Jane Fitzgerald. Nice to meet you.'

'You can call me Derek. I'm so sorry, but I want to hear your views on this Emirates business?'

'If you mean our new status as the Emirates of Britain, I don't think we have the time to have a proper discussion here, do you?' replied Jane, glancing anxiously from her watch to the heavy traffic ahead.

'Erm, as you can see there is a fair bit of traffic ahead because of lane closures so I reckon that gives us at least fifteen minutes,' pressed Derek, nodding at the traffic. He was determined to get the MP's views on the matter. 'What I'm trying to work out is when will they start the persecution and make infidel slaves of us all?'

Jane chuckled. 'I'm sure it won't come to that.'

'Love, I took a bump to the head some time ago, and that left me a little plain, but I'm not completely dense!' said Derek irritably. 'And this is no laughing matter.'

'No, no, you're quite right… but it's not that simple. You see, there is no "*they*" because "*they*" are in fact "*us*". Foreigners didn't take the country — our people did,' said Jane tartly. 'It was white British people — our friends, our parents, our children — who came back from Iraq and did this.' She was surprised to see a grin on Derek's face in his rear-view mirror.

'So one of yours came back a barbarian, then?' he said.

'I'd refrain from using such language — but yes, my son came back Muslim, and he is still a good man,' Jane said softly. 'This country has seen a spike in conversions since the take-over. Some ten percent of the country's population now subscribes to the Islamic faith, according to recent polls.'

They both maintained an awkward silence for a few minutes as they stared at the traffic ahead with throbbing brake lights along Whitehall. Jane pulled some of her papers from her bag but was really just watching the people outside going about their business.

Derek broke the silence. 'Sorry, love, I meant no offence. But how did we end up here like this? I still don't get how it works. Things look the same but it all feels wrong to me.'

'Most people's lives haven't changed; some are even calling the new leaders liberators because of the immediate concessions in welfare and taxation,' said Jane.

'Not sure whose side you're on, but it all sounds too righteous if you ask me,' growled Derek. 'What about cutting off hands for stealing, the stoning of gay folk, killing so-called apostates… the list is endless!'

'I'm not taking sides. I have a job to do, and that's what matters to me…' explained Jane. 'Back to your point on punishments, you won't see any of these for two reasons: firstly, because the emir says that traditions on punishments were often misinterpreted, he adopted the strictest viewpoint… In the case of stoning, well, apparently this has been abrogated in the Qur'an. Even so, that ruling wouldn't apply to any non-Muslim citizen. Secondly, the emir has devolved the management of all non-Muslim affairs to their representatives, the House of Commons in Parliament.'

'So what's that when you're at home, then?' asked Derek, looking a little puzzled.

Jane shuffled through her papers until she pulled out a sheet with colourful diagrams and held it close to the driver protection screen. 'The House of Commons manages the affairs of all non-Muslims, which includes criminal and civil courts, so if *you* were to commit a crime or wanted to raise an issue as a British citizen you would go through the conventional courts or channels,' said Jane, pointing at a red graphic on her sheet. She then pointed to a blue graphic above the red one. 'If, however, you are unhappy with a judgment or outcome, you could petition to a higher authority, the House of Companions. This was previously the old House of Lords, but in most cases they will not interfere.'

'That explains why pubs and other so-called *haraam* businesses are still around, but what about Muslims? I bet they're getting off scot-free?'

'From a Muslim perspective, not really; they are subject to the new Muslim courts under direct control of the House of Companions,' explained Jane, putting her papers away again. 'The emir and his House of Companions do not police worship or dress, but they do not tolerate Muslims committing open *haraam* acts in public that are otherwise ok for non-Muslims.'

'Like what?' probed Derek.

'A person who identifies themselves as Muslim cannot openly drink or run a business that sells alcohol, for instance,' said Jane, looking a little perkier now that they had finally arrived at Parliament Square.

'I see how it works, but it doesn't mean I

wanted it or like it!' cried Derek.

He pulled over near Big Ben and let the MP out; in return she gave him a big tip and told him to stay out of trouble. Derek then sped off with a wary glance at the top of the clock tower; the spire was now crested with a large golden crescent that shimmered under a full moon.

CHAPTER III

Derek sat at home one morning on the thirteenth floor of a council block in East London. He was resting on an old armchair facing a giant flat-screen TV in a near empty living room decorated only with peeling floral wallpaper. He was half chuckling and grunting to himself as he finished scribbling on a notepad spread open on his knees. On a side table nearby was an iPad accompanied by a small wooden frame with headshots of Derek smiling with his late wife. Derek punched a fist in the air in a sign of some sort of victory; he had just finished a song he had been working on since the night before:

> Out, out, out with the emir!
> Down, down, down with his career!
> It can happen, he can go —
> Ask the Spanish, they all know.
> Out, out, out with *shari'ah!*
> Down, down, down with our fear!

It can happen, they can go —
Ask the Greeks, they all know.
Out, out, out with the Muslims!
Down, down, down make 'em swim!
It can happen, they can go —
Ask the Croats, they all know.
Out, out, out with *halal*!
Down, down, down with their *dhal*!
It can happen, they can go —
Ask the Serbs, they all know.

Armed with his song, Derek planned that this was the day he would join others to stand up for his country. Before he left his home, he noticed something on TV that immediately grabbed his attention; it was a rerun of the emir in a live interview by television personality Pete Worgan in front of a live studio audience. Derek felt compelled to sit back down and watch the interview. He raised the volume and watched intently. Both men sat slightly facing each other in formal attire before a lit-up blue backdrop. Following the introductions, the overly confident presenter wasted no time before launching into the questions.

'Let's get down to business, shall we? Emir George, many say you were radicalised, but how would you describe your conversion to Islam?'

'Far from it. Like Sir Winston Churchill and other Victorians of his time, I shared a love for the Orient and Islam from an early age. I was deeply fascinated by Islamic culture and would even dress like an Arab in the comforts of my own home,' replied the emir, smiling.

'Yes, many admire the Islamic culture and its history, and it has helped the world to advance in many disciplines, but what is it precisely that convinced you of its message?' quizzed Worgan.

'Much is speculated about my meetings with this *mysterious* sheikh we captured in Iraq, but the truth is that he directed me to Islam.'

'How exactly?' continued Worgan.

'He saw right through me and spoke to my soul.'

'May I ask what you think he saw?'

'He saw that I was a troubled man looking for peace and absolution.' The emir paused as many in the audience heckled abuse.

'Please continue,' encouraged Worgan softly, raising his hands to calm the audience.

'You see, Pete, I was trying to overcome two struggles. The first was an unabated feeling of emptiness or mundane existence despite the privilege of a good career, wealth and a loving family. The second was the blood I have on my hands for fighting a war that was based on lies.'

'I can understand that many people feel a void in their lives and veterans suffer the guilt of war, but what did this sheikh do for you that a priest or therapist couldn't?'

'The sheikh recited passages from the Qur'an in Arabic that touched my heart in a manner unlike ever before, and when I asked him what he had recited he explained that these were God's words concerning the heart.' The emir put his head down as if recollecting the moment; surprisingly, the studio remained quiet, eager for him to continue. 'The verses explained the maladies of the heart and its remedies… I knew these words were otherworldly and yet they spoke directly to me,' the emir added softly.

'Countless new Muslims have described similar experiences before embracing the Islamic faith, but what the British people want to know is why the coup? Why change Britain?'

'In my mind, to put it simply and honestly, Britain needed a change, the world needed one less bully and my new religion needed a worthy global champion,' said the emir, looking directly into the camera.

A few clapped in the audience but the vast majority booed. Worgan again raised his hands to maintain order before he fired his next question.

'I know the British people, Muslims included, did not ask that you do this on their behalf, and I'm also certain that the global Muslim community did not ask that you become their champion…'

'I was in a very unique position of influence.

Sheikh Ahmed told me of a Prophetic tradition, that a time will come when "the sun will rise from the west". Though this is mainly understood as a physical event in the Islamic eschatology, I'm not the first to believe that this is also symbolic for the rise of Islam in the West,' said the emir.

'So let me get this straight… you think *you* are this sun — or rising star — in the West?'

'No, but this may be start of something good, and the people here and abroad need not be afraid.'

Derek threw his TV remote at the screen. 'What a load of CRAP!' he screamed, before storming out of his flat to make his way to Westminster Palace in his black cab.

When he arrived, he startled a group of anti-emir protesters by parking awkwardly in front of them on Abingdon Street beside the concrete barriers opposite the Victoria Tower entrance. It was sunny with a light breeze, and many tourists hastily passed by, sensing that something ominous was about to happen. He took out a megaphone, climbed on top of his car hugging an effigy of the emir with one arm and then began to sing the song he had worked on earlier from the top of his voice. The song in his cockney accent resembled a terrace chant as it lightly echoed against the buildings around Parliament Square.

The police, who were only yards away,

were immediately on the scene trying unsuccessfully to dissuade Derek from his endeavours. The crowd of protesters began to swell in numbers; some joined in with the song while others took to filming Derek's protest in amusement. Derek, seeing that his antics had garnered some attention, took out a small can of lighter fluid and doused copious amounts of fluid on the head of the effigy. The effigy, a foot shorter than Derek himself, resembled the emir's usual Islamic dress and also had a sign around its neck that read 'Emir George of the Jungle'. Derek set the effigy's head alight and tossed it onto the middle of the road. A number of police officers hurried over to him and pulled him down from the top of this car, pinning him to the ground. Derek shouted and struggled as he was cuffed and dragged into a police van. The crowd, which was booing and cheering to various degrees, followed the van as best as they could as it sped away.

The burning effigy was put out by the firefighters who were on the scene within minutes of the police van pulling away. The crowd were forced to disperse, and all that remained was a trail of black smoke that swirled in the wind.

Following his arrest, Derek made an appearance at the Westminster Magistrates' Court in Central London. He left with a small host of punishments for public order offences including threatening behaviour and nuisance. He had escaped prison — not that the prospect of being locked up bothered him; he was single, self-employed with a reasonable amount of money tucked away for retirement. Instead, he was mortified by a summons by the House of Companions, which was the direct result of protesting against the Islamic state and burning the effigy. He stood outside the magistrates' building, his hands shaking as he contemplated losing them — or worse. He wondered why he was being tried by the Islamic courts, and his mind raced with horrors that included being forced to convert to Islam for clemency. Before leaving for the nearest tube station, a young man in a pinstriped suit stood deliberately in his way, opened a mock-croc briefcase and handed him a business card.

'You have nothing to worry about, Derek. We can help you,' said the man with unshakable confidence. 'Just call me for a meeting and we can discuss how.'

Derek took the card and nodded. He wasn't quite sure what this man could do for him, but thought he would make contact since he had nothing to lose.

CHAPTER IV

A week later, Derek was making his way to an Italian eatery in the Soho district of London's West End. It was a Friday night and revellers busied the streets with noise and merriment. After passing a parade of cafes and restaurants, Derek found the eatery, a warm, welcoming place. Once inside, a waiter directed Derek to a table booked by a David Scholes. The soothing effects of soft lighting, light chatter and a room decorated with rustic wooden beams calmed Derek's nerves as he navigated through tables to get to one in a corner where two men sat waiting for him.

David Scholes was the one of the men Derek had met a week ago straight after the court hearing; he looked as corporate as ever, dressed in another pinstriped suit. The other man was Mediterranean in appearance, and he was dressed in a loose *thobe* and a white *taqiyah*. He had a large black beard and this unsettled Derek who had not expected to see a second person there, particularly one that resembled a Muslim.

'Who is he?' said Derek suspiciously, not taking a seat.

'His name is Majid. He is a friend,' replied David softly.

Derek was not convinced and remained standing. 'Bet he can't even speak English!' he spat, slowly backing away.

'Of course I can, now please sit down,' Majid said calmly, his accent unfamiliar to Derek's ears. 'We all want the same thing…' He glanced at David for support.

'Yes, Derek, it is in your interest to stay,' added David. 'We are both here to help you and your country.'

'Ok, but I don't trust *him*,' Derek said warily, finally sitting down. He wasted no time and began to browse through the menu and wine list.

David placed food orders for everyone on the table; this included a wine order for Derek and himself.

Derek sneered at Majid. 'Not drinking?'

'No, it is forbidden for Muslims.'

'So should you even be here?' asked Derek.

'Muslim movements to these places aren't restricted, but their proprietors are prohibited from selling alcohol to Muslims — otherwise they suffer huge fines. In fact, they should check our new ID cards, which state our religion.' Majid held up a card resembling a driver's license.

'I know. I think you'll find that we all have one of those now,' said Derek, rolling his eyes.

'The point is we both represent two powerful nations that want the UK back to the way it was,' interjected David, 'and through your antics a great opportunity has presented itself.'

'Erm, I thought this would have been paradise for our Majid here!' Derek mumbled through a mouthful of complimentary bread.

Majid, turning slightly red, took out a file from underneath the table and presented it to Derek. Inside it were photos and documents littered with official logos and stamps. 'Those I represent do not believe this to be a true Islamic state,' he said. 'They have deviated from the true teachings of the Qur'an and Prophetic tradition. They've even set up a new Islamic legal school, calling it the *Anglo Madhab*!'

'Boring. But I get it…' Derek leant his head forward over the table towards Majid. 'You just don't like Muslim women working or driving or not wearing a veil. You have a problem with Anglo-Islam — or, I should say, British Islam.'

'More like hippie Islam — but the fact remains that this state is an affront to other Muslim states and should be removed to restore Britain back to its former glory and old alliances,' said a flustered Majid, again glancing towards David for support.

'Are *they* not buying your oil?' quipped Derek, sipping his glass of wine with some satisfaction.

'Derek, your recent protest has shown us your bravery. We know you would be happy to risk all to take back your country.' David paused as the waiter arrived with their dishes. 'Your pending summons is actually a rare occasion where you will have the opportunity to voice your concerns to the emir directly. It's the third summons of which we've become aware — we cannot miss it!'

Derek raised his eyebrows. 'Wow! So I'm not in trouble? Keep going…'

'You're not in trouble, no — quite the opposite. The emir meets selected individuals with grievances against the state and endeavours to resolve them.'

'How *noble* of him,' mocked Majid. 'He thinks he's Umar bin al-Khattab!'

'Since you will be meeting him face to face, you are in an excellent position to dispose of him indefinitely,' David continued.

Derek shuddered and drained his wine glass, which David immediately topped up. Derek thought for a moment, and then whispered, 'You m-mean an assassination!'

'This is an opportune moment, Derek — one that will place you in the history books forever.'

'It's ironic, but a *nobody* like you is in a

better position to do this than any foreign agent,' said Majid, chuckling.

Derek looked at his empty plate and then gave a slow nod. 'I love my country… Maybe my empty life has been gearing me up for this moment.'

'It won't be difficult. You just have to feign the acceptance of the emir's arguments, accept Islam so the emir can embrace you as a brother,' cried David, unable to contain his excitement.

'And that's how you will do it — he won't go instantly so you will be able to leave safely without raising any suspicion whatsoever,' said Majid.

'Do *what* exactly?' asked Derek, a little hesitant with the thought of things going wrong.

'We'll do the hard part, co-ordinating with defectors in the emir's House of Companions and so on,' said Majid. 'Your part in the game is simple: you must grow a bushy beard and moustache for your summons in three months. In the meantime we will fashion a miniscule device that can sit discreetly between your chin and lower lip so you can carry out the mission.'

'What will it do?'

'When you embrace the emir, your device will inject poison into his neck; he will think it nothing more than a scratch from the bristles of your coarse beard and then he will be dead within a few short hours.'

'You'll have to hug him tight to get into the right position to inject the poison,' added David.

'I'll do it!' said Derek. 'I'm actually no stranger to death or strange bodily devices, but how will this get our old Britain back?'

'You cut the head off the snake, and we'll do the rest!' replied Majid, standing up and extending his right hand over the table.

Derek shook it.

CHAPTER V

Three months later, Derek's summons date arrived. As planned, he had grown a beard that hid most of his face and a device containing poison, which was essentially a tiny pill with a short syringe at the end of it. Majid and David had worked tirelessly over the past few months, trialling many variations of the device to get the balance right, not compromising a miniscule size that injected successfully upon light impact.

Derek arrived early at the summons venue, the British Museum, where he reported to the information desk for his appointment with the emir. A comely woman in business attire appeared within seconds and escorted Derek to the entrance of the Reading Room through an empty central courtyard. Derek admired the floor of white marble under a tessellated glass roof until he had to walk through a body scanner followed by a pat down by security staff in military uniform. His racing heart calmed as he cleared the pat down; the beard was left untouched and his gold earring gave the device's metal syringe the necessary cover. The woman then escorted Derek into the centre of the Reading Room, where the emir stood waiting for him between two empty chairs. A large bloodhound with a beautiful black-and-tan coat lay still on the floor beside him. The hound suddenly sprang to life, growling viciously, gnashing its teeth at Derek as he approached cautiously. The emir signalled for the woman to take the hound away, which she did without any trouble. He then approached Derek, shook his hand and ushered him to sit on the nicer of the two chairs. A few security men stood a short distance behind the emir whilst a small army of them were stationed around the room, motionless like waxworks.

'Welcome, Derek, it's lovely to see you again. Sorry about my old friend Henry over there, he is somewhat overprotective... You're not here to hurt me, are you?'

'Of course not — I'm no terrorist! And what do you mean "again"?' mumbled Derek, confused.

'I recognised you from the YouTube footage of your protest – I first saw you when I visited you in hospital after your accident,' replied the emir, patiently waiting for Derek to sit down.

'Ah, you're good...' Derek laughed, still

standing. 'I heard about how you mess with people's heads! Anyway, why visit me in hospital?'

'Sadly, there were some casualties in our fight to take over; I visited most of the survivors in hospital. You may not recall this, but your accident was the result of a stray bullet from your fellow countrymen who fought against us — it took out one of your tyres…'

Derek suddenly felt he had been transported back to that very moment in time — a drive along the Embankment on a grey afternoon disturbed by sudden claps of thunder, followed by smoke everywhere. Only there was no rain… instead, people were screaming and running in all directions. His vehicle suddenly lost control…

Trembling, Derek sank into his seat, weighed down by memories.

They sat in silence for a short moment as Derek gathered his thoughts. The emir looked very much at home in the grand room surrounded by desks and large book stacks all under a huge dome. He was a tall man in his late forties, and his athletic frame was encased in a tweed three-piece suit. His trimmed beard and blend of flowing platinum-blond hair shone in the light coming from lamps on the reading desks around the circular room. The emir could very easily have passed as a headmaster with a kind face and worried eyes, squinting as if in the sunlight. Derek began to relax until a maroon cravat around the emir's neck caught his eye – *damn it*, he thought — *this will derail my plan unless it is removed somehow*. The emir broke the silence, seeing that Derek had become uncomfortable.

'Please do not be nervous – you have nothing to be worried about.'

'Not worried,' lied Derek, trying to get the cravat out of his head. The emir didn't look like a man who dabbled in much small talk and got straight into the matter at hand.

'I invited you today so I can hear your concerns. What is upsetting you, Derek?'

Derek pulled out his ID card and held it up. 'I'm a reluctant citizen of this terrorist state, and it breaks my heart and angers me that you have taken my country away from me,' said Derek with a grimace, returning the card back into his coat pocket.

'The ID card is merely a small requirement to verify who you are. We no longer keep tabs on our citizens through surveillance, and spy agencies are a thing of the past.'

'But what about my country?!'

'Your country — or I should say *our* country — remains much the same. The vast majority of the British institutions are running in accordance to previous principles and practices. The only major reform I have made is to convert the outdated House of Lords to the new House of Companions, which merely exists to ensure that the House of Commons governs you fairly. So what specifically angers you, Derek?'

'You've changed a lot of things in this country!' cried Derek. 'We've lost our British identity, you've made Muslims of my kinsmen, people are afraid to do what they want… the list goes on!'

The emir reached behind him, grabbed a file and flicked through a few pages. 'You were a single man with no family, earning a decent wage as a black cabby before the horrible accident, no?'

'Yes — and?'

'You are much the same person now living your life as determined by you — as an atheist man, restored to good health, paying less tax, I believe, thanks to our reforms. So, what specifically do you take issue with?'

'Yes, but you are controlling our previous leader, and we didn't get a choice, and you may not be foreign but your ideas aren't British, and —'

'I understand, Derek, I do… but do you know why I chose this venue?' asked the emir serenely.

'Why?'

'It has been used by great people who were once considered radicals and revolutionaries, but they gave us ideas that have benefited the world even to this day,' said the emir, standing up then pacing slowly with hands behind his back. 'You see, this country — like any other great nation — has benefited from the influence of foreign invaders. Take, for instance, what the Romans and the Normans did for us.'

'Yeah, but where was *my* choice in all this?! I wanted something better for this country, not bloody Islam!'

'I lived and breathed to serve my country, but when I was in Iraq I realised that we have to answer for all the turmoil we have created in the world. The ailment our country suffers is not from foreign lands but from within. Sometimes protecting a country means one has to protect it from itself.'

'So you forcefully took over?!' Derek said incredulously.

'Yes, Derek, I stepped in — and I would do it again if I had to. Under my rule you are safe, you will never starve, you will never be cast out on to the street if you can't pay rent,' said the emir, sitting back down and focusing on Derek. 'Please tell me, Derek, what is really the cause of your anger? What drove you to burn the effigy?'

Derek simply glared.

'Why are you so angry?' repeated the emir. 'It pains me to see that you are very upset.'

'I don't need your pity,' said Derek, cowering away from the concern in the emir's gaze. It was as if his squinting blue eyes were peering into his soul. 'W-What makes you think there are other reasons?'

'I sense that I may not be the source of your anger entirely, and that there may be other underlying issues.'

'A-Alright! I'm alone, ok?!' cried Derek, shaking with sadness and anger. 'And this whole thing has made me lonelier than ever before!' He broke down and sobbed with his face buried in his hands.

Emir George darted forward, put a gentle hand on Derek's shoulder and offered him his cravat. 'I'm so sorry, I don't have a handkerchief.'

'I'm a lonely bloke, that's what it is,' admitted Derek. 'I'm also angry with the last Government for letting this happen — I feel betrayed by them, by you, by EVERYONE!'

'We can help you with this — you don't have to be alone!' said the emir, gently helping Derek to his feet. 'Please, join our community of believers, accept Islam… we offer family, a sense of belonging and purpose — things your current representatives struggle to give you and even themselves.'

'I think you're a good man, but I can't do it!' cried Derek, looking afraid.

'Of course you can — it's simple,' said the emir, with a beaming smile. 'The *shahada,* or declaration of faith, is the first step. The rest can come slowly!'

Derek nodded and slowly repeated the *shahada* after his leader. Emir George wiped a tear from his own cheek, apparently moved by the moment. Derek knew what he had to do but struggled to understand why he felt like aborting the mission.

As expected, the emir locked Derek in a long embrace, welcoming the new believer. Derek tiptoed ever so slightly so his chin could make light contact with the emir's long neck. The device successfully hit its mark in an instant and released its toxins into the emir's bloodstream with him being none the wiser.

A little later, Derek left the emir, having agreed to meet a whole network of contacts to learn about his new faith. Far from feeling like he had completed a monumental mission that would change the course of world history, Derek left crestfallen with an unwelcome sense of remorse.

In the days that followed, Derek watched a glum series of events unfold from the safety of a secret house provided by David and Majid. He cared not to admit that the assassination of the emir felt like an affliction on his constitution and it was something he would have to learn to live with.

EPILOGUE

A year on, Derek sat in the outside area of a busy café somewhere in the Mediterranean region sipping an ice-cold beverage and reading a British newspaper. The headline on the front page read: 'Britain without Emir George — One Year On'. The piece briefly described how the Islamic state had fallen following the death of its leader. It mentioned how five nations with careful planning had disabled the country's security systems and then launched a successful assault with the help of ex-servicemen who had not joined the Companions. The state had surrendered its arms to minimise civilian casualties, but one year on Britain still grappled with a new identity as a country free from the emirates — a country now home to a growing number of indigenous Muslims who made up a tenth of the country's overall population.

Derek recalled with some discomfort a recent tabloid piece he had read about the assassination. It had marked the day as 'St Derek's Day'. It had also cited some of the emir's last words to his followers; he requested that they forgive his murderer, who was just a loner who no one cared to visit during an entire year in hospital.

The Islamic call to prayer suddenly interrupted Derek's thoughts. He put his paper down and loosened a cravat around his neck — the maroon one the emir had let him keep over a year ago. Derek then left some money on the table and joined a crowd of people making their way towards the call.

SADHEK KHAN was born in London in 1978. He finished his studies at the University of the Arts, London and started working in the welfare-to-work industry as an employment coach. He developed his experience in the voluntary, private and public sectors, and he remains active in the public health sector.

As a Muslim, and having lived and worked in the East End, Khan has first-hand experience of the struggles faced by second-generation Muslims from immigrant backgrounds living in deprived areas. This coupled with questions surrounding Muslim identities in Western societies prompted Khan to write *The Emirates of Britain*, satirically exploring the right-wing politics of a perceived Muslim takeover.

Publisher Information

Rowanvale Books provides publishing services to independent authors, writers and poets all over the globe. We deliver a personal, honest and efficient service that allows authors to see their work published, while remaining in control of the process and retaining their creativity. By making publishing services available to authors in a cost-effective and ethical way, we at Rowanvale Books hope to ensure that the local, national and international community benefits from a steady stream of good quality literature.

For more information about us, our authors or our publications, please get in touch.

www.rowanvalebooks.com
info@rowanvalebooks.com

Rowanvale
Books

Lightning Source UK Ltd.
Milton Keynes UK
UKOW03f2057250417
299899UK00004B/165/P